AS THE CROW FLIES

As the crow flies

Véronique Tadjo

Translated from the French by Wangũi wa Goro

PENGUIN BOOKS

PENGUIN BOOKS

Published by the Penguin Group
Penguin Books (South Africa) (Pty) Ltd, 24 Sturdee Avenue, Rosebank,
Johannesburg 2196, South Africa
Penguin Group (USA) Inc, 375 Hudson Street, New York, New York 10014,
USA
Penguin Group (Canada), 90 Eglinton Avenue East, Suite 700, Toronto,
Ontario, Canada M4P 2Y3 (a division of Pearson Penguin Canada Inc)
Penguin Books Ltd, 80 Strand, London WC2R 0RL, England
Penguin Ireland, 25 St Stephen's Green, Dublin 2, Ireland (a division of
Penguin Books Ltd)
Penguin Group (Australia), 250 Camberwell Road, Camberwell, Victoria
3124, Australia (a division of Pearson Australia Group Pty Ltd)
Penguin Books India Pvt Ltd, 11 Community Centre, Panchsheel Park, New
Delhi – 110 017, India
Penguin Group (NZ), 67 Apollo Drive, Mairangi Bay, Auckland 1310, New
Zealand (a division of Pearson New Zealand Ltd)

Penguin Books (South Africa) (Pty) Ltd, Registered Offices:
24 Sturdee Avenue, Rosebank, Johannesburg 2196, South Africa

www.penguinbooks.co.za

Original title: À Vol d'Oiseau
Copyright © text Véronique Tadjo 2001
Copyright © this translation Wangũi wa Goro 2008

First published by Heinemann Educational Publishers 1992
This edition published by Penguin Books (South Africa) (Pty) Ltd 2008
Under licence from Pearson Education Limited

ISBN: 978 0 143 02622 8

Typeset by Nix Design in 11/14 pt Life
Cover designed by mr design
Printed and bound by Paarl Print, Cape Town

Message from Chinua Achebe:

Africa is a huge continent with a diversity of cultures and languages. Africa is not simple – often people want to simplify it, generalise it, stereotype its people, but Africa is very complex. The world is just starting to get to know Africa. The last five hundred years of European contact with Africa produced a body of literature that presented Africa in a very bad light and now the time has come for Africans to tell their own stories.

The Penguin African Writers Series will bring a new energy to the publication of African literature. Penguin Books (South Africa) is committed to publishing both established and new voices from all over the African continent to ensure African stories reach a wider global audience.

This is really what I personally want to see – writers from all over Africa contributing to a definition of themselves, writing ourselves and our stories into history. One of the greatest things literature does is allow us to imagine; to identify with situations and people who live in completely different circumstances, in countries all over the world. Through this series, the creative exploration of those issues and experiences that are unique to the African consciousness will be given a platform, not only throughout Africa, but also to the world beyond its shores.

Storytelling is a creative component of human experience and in order to share our experiences with the world, we as Africans need to recognise the importance of our own stories. By starting the series on the solid foundations laid by the renowned Heinemann African Writers Series, I am honoured to join Penguin in inviting young and upcoming writers to accept the challenge passed down by celebrated African authors of earlier decades and to continue to explore, confront and question the realities of life in Africa through their work; challenging Africa's people to lift her to her rightful place among the nations of the world.

Chinua Achebe

If you want to love
Do so
To the ends of the earth
With no shortcuts
Do so
As the crow flies.

Indeed, I too would have loved to write one of those serene stories with a beginning and an end. But as you know only too well, it is never like that. Lives mingle, people tame one another and part. Destinies are lost.

On looking at your reflection in the mirror you say, 'I don't like what I see.' You are hurt by your weaknesses. You are hurt by your failures.

Listen. If you cannot stand the thought of your rotting body when you are buried under the earth, or if you are able to say: 'I don't want to rot, please burn me!' then you will be allowing the flowers of freedom to blossom. Your strength will spring from your scattered weaknesses and with your common humanity you will fight against the ills erected as royal edifices over dunes of silence.

ONE

I

He was a magnificent man with hands that smiled at anyone who knew how to look at them. His long fingers and the beauty of his gestures evoked poetry. But what made you dream was the rhythmic lilt in the tone of his voice and its ability to both speak and empathise.

He had an unusual way of looking at you and a unique way of carrying himself. His whole force lay in his neck.

He lived in one of those houses with a pointed roof, white windows and red brick walls. A small garden ran down to the road.

The man was rich. Rich in his life. Rich in his family. You could hear the children's laughter fill the atmosphere and decorate the home. This was a world apart.

They met at the airport. She had travelled a long way and he came to pick her up as planned. On the way to the house, he pointed out the city's monuments. She admired their beauty but did not say much.

When he opened the door, she found the house infused with joy. She greeted everyone while he went to deposit her luggage in one of the rooms. That evening, the food was prepared with particular care. They had brought out a white tablecloth.

She immediately liked her room. The bed was comfortable. There were green houseplants standing on the floor and a window overlooked the garden. She noticed a barbecue outside. A child's bicycle leant against a tree.

The next day they arranged to eat outdoors. Some friends came over to join them. It was a beautiful day with the sun shining high in the sky. As she watched him light the fire, she knew that she was going to love him.

She craved for him every day. At night after closing the door, when she was on her own, she could hear sounds drifting from the room above. She listened attentively to their footsteps and she could hear taps running and the bath water draining away. When sleep eluded her, she would read until she dropped off, the pages still open.

She spent those days walking about in the city, and watching him busy in his workshop. She loved to watch him in silence, watch the agility of his hands as they handled the wood, caressing it and moulding it into multiple shapes.

One morning she wrote the following words on a piece of paper which she handed to him: 'I'm desperately in love with you.' On reading it, he burst out laughing and she knew she had won.

After that, everything happened quickly. At first they saw each other alone in town. Then, they spent the afternoons together. Every evening they arrived home separately. On occasions he would reach the house before her and, at other times, she would. Her heart would always leap when, on approaching the house, she found his car parked in front of the gate.

Often, from her little room, she could hear what sounded like loud voices, which would startle her from sleep and make her temples throb like drums. She thought she could hear heavy footsteps coming down the staircase and that, at any moment, the door would burst open …

However, the evenings were quiet. The shouting was coming from the television. The warm nights pearled the sheets in sweat.

As time was in no hurry, she busied herself helping the children with their homework. She would pore over it making corrections and reading exercise books covered in childish scrawls. Sometimes, she would go on walks with his wife. They were both fond of nature and spent long hours admiring the flowers, resplendent in the summer sunshine.

As time went by over the weeks that passed, they became close. They planned meals together and shared the chores. They seemed like friends.

But one day, she had had enough of the whole sickening situation. Sleepless nights assailed her. She had no idea where to turn. She had to leave this house and never return. The town had become a prison and her visit a complete failure. She felt trapped, diminished, hurt. She could no longer put up with the lonely nights. She had had enough of those smiles to which she could not respond, tired of not being able to demonstrate how she felt.

She decided to make this their last date. In the hotel room, they bade each other farewell.

Why on earth did it have to be on that particular day? Why on earth did his wife have to see them leaving that place?

It looks as though the house is now up for sale. She has won the divorce and she gets to keep the children.

II

It was a sordid affair. You were told not to go back there. You should have moved away from that town or neighbourhood. Why repeat the same thing? What were you hoping for? You knew deep inside that there was nothing to be gained, that all

4

had been said, and that, at the end of it all, you were well and truly past the best of it. Anyway, what good would it do you? You had a choice.

It was a sordid affair right from the start. Some unlikely love story that would come to nothing. He came, you saw him, and it did not work. It was over, so why did you go back?

You told yourself, 'We'll see ... we'll be friends.' However, the only thing that remained as before was the tension, this floating lie. The memory that had no urge to fade.

For you, of course, it was spent. Sometimes, you remembered, but things were no longer the same. The days had changed. Even the city seemed insipid with its white buildings and well-manicured gardens.

You drifted through time as though your sleep was crumbling. You lost faith. What haunted you was the waiting. Tomorrow, everything would start all over again. You would be back and then there would be nothing. Nothing at all.

The waiting was tough. Intolerable. When the other one came, it felt like a plunge into the sea. You felt a breeze, blowing. Your heart surged. A flicker still lingered, after all.

But you had been told: it was a sordid affair. No longer room for fine sentiments. Just a time of resentment. Harsh words uttered. Disappointments.

You see, you should never have returned. There are no fresh mornings, just torpid nights.

Sometimes, you feel as though it had never really happened, that all that had been something else. You wanted it to be just the two of you. But you see, right from the start, it was a sordid affair.

III

Such a strong desire, that it burned my house, ravaged all my fields, and extended all the way to the forest. All that was left was the strong pounding of my heart. The future had deleted that page.

Nothing existed but this moment, this festive atmosphere. Garlands hung on the sky walls. Nothing, but my spirit moving up a notch to another story that had nothing to do with ours, the kind of tale whose source is unknown.

It reminded you of those stormy nights caught in the rain. The glistening sound of the first drops; then, after that, it felt like a downpour sweeping everything in its way, the bending trees, the fleeing shadows, and the smell of the earth.

Anyway, tomorrow could have been a fine day. It could have been a day spent at the seaside with the sun soothing the skin. You would have found me beautiful, and I would have told the winds my dreams of a thousand and one nights.

IV

I remember that laughter which had my soul in stitches. It was like the luminous fresh rain that banished all boredom, the fleeting days, and the winter of the heart.

All I wanted was to hang on to what was beautiful but terrible thoughts keep knocking on my memory; the kinds of thoughts that are best discarded. I keep remembering the night when we spoke, when words were finding it hard to escape my lips and each syllable hampered the clarity of meaning. I asked you questions that needed an answer. And each time the sentences were punctuated by silence. A hurricane in my chest.

I cannot stop thinking that life might have missed a step, and that something was wrong. Strong words uttered too late, hurled into space. Lost for all time.

V

I must leave. You see, I want a different world. Things have changed. I search for you and all I find is your shadow. All of a sudden, your scent is too strong. Your estranged body has lost its heat.

Today I am waiting at an airport where most of the travellers are couples. I have the whole afternoon ahead of me. The plane is delayed. I have lost all track of time.

I am dressed in my nice outfit, and I am wearing the earrings you bought me. I shift my ring to another finger. There, at the tip of the horizon, at another airport, someone is waiting for me.

VI

A ghetto. In a large city in the United States of America. Washington DC. A black man. He must get out of it ... At all costs.

I read in the papers that a man killed his whole family. Cut each one up into small pieces: father, mother and younger sister. *This is a bad neighbourhood.* Mauvais quartier.

The bus is filthy. The seats are torn. In the street, young men hang about waiting. For what? They seem ... not very ... sort of, poor. In the women's toilet at Howard University, I figured out the graffiti: My man is a freak, My nigger is hot.

In Washington, squirrels hopping about in the city centre take me by surprise. They are the hope of a still beautiful city. Every morning, a bird perches on the windowsill. It has a blue tail.

The parks are covered in a thick lawn; the gardens are in bloom. A black man passes by, a radio glued to his ear. He is listening to WHUR. This is music country. I shop, eat, sleep, think in music. Michael Jackson's 'Thriller', Donna Summer's 'She Works Hard For The Money', ring in my head.

I am afraid of getting fat. The ice creams are gigantic, and corn-flakes honey-coated. Canned laughter and applause on the box.

Washington is peaceful. You can occasionally hear the siren of an ambulance wailing on deserted Sunday streets. A helicopter hovers over the area. Its searchlights slice the darkness. They are looking for a man.

The city seems beautiful. The White House is white. Dozens more drug dealers have been locked up: grass, cocaine, heroin.

Bus 36 takes me home.

VII

There are no frontiers.

TWO

VIII

Muddy, muddy Macory. I see snotty-nosed kids tumbling about streets covered in black mud. I see trousers rolled up, shoes held in hands, wrappers raised to the knee. I see bare feet, dirtied by the battered earth. Taxis are immobilised in the middle of pools of water.

I see a group of children waiting for cars to get stuck. Their torsos are bare and the rain waters them like wild plants.

Muddy, muddy Macory. I see a city suffering from its ills. I see the compounds, eating places, bars, prostitutes, bad guys.

I see a woman making aloco. The oil, hot. The plantains turn brown. Her feet are covered in dirt. Smoke stings her eyes. A kid waits his turn. He has five francs. That can buy you three alocos.

An Abogi boils water next to a table where pieces of bread are displayed. Two men sit eating in silence.

I see a dog. He is covered in fleas. He rummages in the garbage.

It gets dark. I see a man bathing, his back glimmering in the shadow like a climbing liana. His vigorous gestures make the water resound in countless splashes.

The Anagos have lit their hurricane lamps. The market looks like an assembly of sorcerers.

It is warm and dark and I think of Akissi.

Being pregnant is not something she had contemplated. It is too late now. She must conceal it. In the compound she has to ignore the women's probing eyes. These do not bother her as much as her mother's penetrating glare that pierces her thoughts and invades her sleep.

Every day she can feel her breasts swelling, her whole body transform. She has become a different person. She does not understand this thing, which has lodged itself in her, draining all her energies. She is not ready for this.

The local nurse had proved to be quite incompetent. He had promised her that the injections would return her body to its normal state but nothing had happened.

The place that her friend told her about is not hard to find. It is a shack erected in the middle of a disused sawmill. You can still smell sawdust floating in the air. The city sounds seem to resonate from far away. She puts her hand in her pocket and clutches the borrowed money tightly in her fingers. She will not need to speak to the man. All she has to do is hand over the bundle of crumpled notes.

Evening falls. She looks at the darkening sky. Around her, the faces of the waiting women are stony masks. She sits down. When her turn comes, she gets up without a word.

She cannot see very well. The room looks dirty. She is assailed by the smell of blood. The freshness of the harmattan has faded. The man's hands are moist and precise.

The pain is blinding. Profound. She gets up. Her head reels. She throws up.

Muddy, muddy Macory. I see the neighbourhood gangs. These boys have already turned into men. Their names are Hendrix, Pepito, Johnny, and they have a small band.

THREE

IX

You should listen to those whose voices remain unheard although the wisdom they carry is shaped by their closeness to the earth. No refined language but the pace of life at a gallop refashions outmoded images, well-worn phrases, and ways of thinking that are out of date.

There is a story in each of us. Listen, somebody is speaking:

'It is three o'clock. I will be late. I have just half an hour to get across town. This bus not arriving will get me in trouble. Rehearsals tire me. It is the same every day, at the same time. Today it is the second act. I go on stage. I represent the people. Symbolically. I do many things. I till. I fish. I cast my net high. I hunt. I dance. The drum beats loudly and rhythmically. My feet step in time. Chest stiffened, neck arched. Then, 'Stop,' my arms are stretched outwards like a cross. The hero is fighting for me, against the monarch.

I do not really understand everything. He often explains all the acts to us, though. We also discuss things in groups. Still, I don't understand.

It is hot. I am dripping with sweat. My head aches. I will miss the warming-up exercises. He must pay me back my bus fare. I have to tell Him about my accommodation problems. I do not want to live in this compound any more. It's too noisy. The toilet door is broken and it stinks.

The area is huge yet I don't know anybody. People come here for sleeping. In the morning, when the sun rises, the bus stop looks like a market place.

When I think of the last play we performed, it hurts. It is very depressing. I don't feel like going to rehearsals. If it wasn't for Him, I would stop going. He is counting on all of us, though. Yesterday He told us not to worry, that we were professionals and that our time will come. He said, 'Don't worry, just keep playing so that at least the hire of the room can be paid.'

Me, I just wanted to cry. When I look at the others, they look like they are about to cry also. After all that work! The room was empty. Only three rows full. We waited until 9.15, then 9.30 and then 10 o'clock. Somebody came to the door and asked, 'Hey, is it going to begin or not?'

Then He said: 'We have to perform. It is okay. That will teach you to perform no matter what the circumstances. That's how you will gain experience.' But me, my throat was tight, and when the curtain opened, I felt like I was going to die. I felt unabled to move. But in the end, I performed. We played, the people laughed and that made me a bit pleased. They clapped. They were happy.

We too were happy in the end. He gave us a bit of money, which He asked that we share out amongst ourselves. After that, we went to talk to the spectators. I like that. They asked us questions. Some of them were kind.

As for me, I was speaking to a girl. She asked me if being an actor was tough. Then all of a sudden, we heard shouting. I thought that the people were just messing about, but the shouting went on for a long time and it was even impossible for us to go on talking. We went to see what was happening. Even me, I was shocked by what I saw. Two youths sat on the ground, completely naked except for their underwear. They were the ones we could hear screaming, yelling. They were putting their hands on their heads to stop the stick from hitting them on the shoulders and backs. One of them was shouting: 'Forgive us, sir, forgive us.' The beating got harder and harder. The other one was crying and his mouth was twisted as he kicked his feet about. The girl standing next to me asked:

'But what's going on? Why are you beating them?'

He turned suddenly and looked at her straight.

'They are thugs. Thiefs! They were caught breaking into a car in the parking area. They stole everything: papers, radio, cassettes. Everyone is scared now. That is why nobody comes to the theatre any more!' But the girl went on when He began hitting them again:

'Stop it! You're going to injure them!'

'Don't stick your nose in things that don't concern you, it's none of your business!'

The girl made a face and left. We too felt sorry for them because He was so big and strong. But He kept whacking them, and there was nothing we could do. He was angry and you could tell that no matter what we said, He was going to take it out on the two youths. Somebody went to call the police. We stood around Him and begged for mercy on behalf of the thieves. He got angry again. He whacked them harder. Towards one o'clock in the morning, the police came. He went with them to report the robbery.

It is hot. That bus is not coming. If the new play works, that will be great. That should make a bit of money. As you know, acting is not a real job. One day you are lucky and another day you are not. I love it but it is not a real job. What is good about it is that we get to travel. We perform around the country. That way, I know many towns. Sometimes we stay in hotels and sometimes we stay in people's houses. He said that maybe we would go to France one day. France ... I have seen it in the cinema and on television, but that will be great, if we go to France. I will buy lots of stuff. They say you can find all sorts of things over there. Then we can earn some money. I know a guy who made it as an actor in Paris. I saw a picture of him in a magazine the other day. He looked smart and there was a white girl next to him. He had his arm round her shoulder and he was smiling.

My friends say that my acting is good. Anyway, He is happy with me. He says that I am making good progress. I have to keep doing it, no matter what.

I left school early. I did not study to become an actor. I was just hanging around, not doing anything special. One day He called me. At the time, He lived near the police station. I knew Him because I had seen pictures of Him in the papers. I also knew that we are from the same place back home. His village is near my mother's one. Everybody in the neighbourhood knows His name.

His house is always full of people. The drummers from the group sleep at His house. Sometimes there are a few actors there too. Anyway, the place is always crowded. They eat together and if you are around at lunchtime, you can join in the meal too. The girls cook rice and stew. In the morning He gives them money to go to the market.

He writes and directs the plays Himself, and we perform. In town, they say that He is a good producer. When He speaks on television, His French is good. He usually talks with people from the university. They say that He is a revolutionary and that the plays we perform say bad things about the government. We always get into trouble. At times, when rehearsals finish, we are not even sure if we are going to perform or not.

One day, after we had performed at the theatre just three times, the minister called Him. After that, we could not perform any more. He got angry. There were pictures of Him in the newspapers and He spoke on the radio. We had to stop the performing. That year, we did not do a thing. He called us and told us that we had nothing to fear and that if there were any problems, He would deal with them. He asked us to stay at home. We will see what will happen in a few weeks' time.

Things were much better when His wife was around. She was kind. She always gave good advice. She knew everything that went on, but she hated it that the house was always full with people. One day she came back from work and kicked everyone who was there out of the house. Because of this, He went off to stay at His brother's house for one month.

I agree with what His wife did, although it is not a good thing to kick people out like that. I would personally never go to live with married people. It causes too much palaver. Now because His wife is gone away, the house belongs to everybody. They never lock the door. You can come and go, as you like. If He is not around, you can stay. In any case, there is nothing to steal. He has a TV, but it does not work.

So, the day when He called me and asked me whether I wanted to act, I said, 'Yes.' That is how I got involved.

In the play, I represent the people. My hands are stretched in the form of a cross. Symbolically. The hero is fighting for me. Fighting against the monarch.'

Four

X

We must be living in a squalid century. He begs because he is an albino. Another man has drawn his sleeve well back in order to show his stump to effect. He also wears shorts to let people see his rotten leg.

The shop fronts light up the subdued city. The night hides its boredom behind blinding neon lights. You want a classical round watch with a leather strap and there is no shortage of choice. I am dazzled.

This must be a century that is ill at ease. My friend wants to die. Several days pass without my seeing her, and on my return, I tell her, 'You shouldn't take things so seriously. Life is not a soap opera like *Dallas*. You must learn to cope.'

Sometimes I wonder: 'Why must we make the same mistakes as our parents and grandparents? We play Russian roulette with our lives, as if we have nothing to lose.'

Time moves anticlockwise and somersaults backwards. Will our children be able to avoid our mistakes? Will they know how to judge us?

XI

Give me a few more days and you will see what I will do. The same thing. I feel it already. I have seen it in his eyes, in his hand, the way he walks and the way he smiles. I already know it.

If time was on our side, we would have smashed down walls, forced doors open, ripped roofs and shattered windows. Rain would have soaked the soil and the wind would have howled in the middle of the ruins.

I felt it in the way he speaks and in the force which draws me to him. The call extends way beyond the mountains, and beyond the seas. It is like a powerful drum deafening my body.

But today, time is not on our side and days elude us. Our lives run on parallel tracks ...

Would you have desired me if we had walked similar paths?

XII

The story of misery recounts itself. Years pass by and nothing changes. It is almost always the same old never-ending tale. Dirty, muddy roads and blackened walls.

I want to talk about the death of a pregnant woman in that suffocating part of the city. The architect had not been entirely honest and the contractor was negligent. It was in low-cost housing. Gas had built up in the plumbing and travelled up the toilet pipes and into the houses.

Did you know that Turkish toilets could kill? Why Turkish and not Chinese ones? Those WC things kill. I can prove it: my wife is dead.

The husband in tears says: 'We live in a world where we can tell neither head nor tail. We live in a world that jeers at you and proffers insults, an incestuous world that robs you of hope. I tell you my wife died in that stagnant neighbourhood. You'll never have me believe that the gods' wrath caused it!'

The buses are so full of passengers they have nearly reached bursting point. People are warned through the television: 'Beware of men who claim to multiply banknotes. They are charlatans. They will steal your money and fade into thin air.'

Abortions are illegal. You will get to learn. Young girls, muttering inaudible words, contort their bodies on the hospital floor. One of them looks especially young. When a nurse passes in the corridor, her groans grow louder.

Someone told me the following story, which I will recount to you as I heard it.

FIVE

XIII

The town was at the mercy of the sky. Nobody knew where to run. Clothes clung on to bodies. Sweat rolled down broken backs, blurred the pedestrians' vision and made every being smell of the earth. The rains were late in coming. The sun had definitely decided to show itself in its full glory. It made the inhabitants speak in hushed tones, and hurry so as not to be found lingering in the scorching heat. The tall trees wilted in the dense atmosphere.

But when the evening announced itself and the first breaths of cool air descended on the city, men gathered in large and boisterous clusters. Crowds of people dispersed in all directions. You could hear the staccato pounding of pestles. Smoke rose slowly from the courtyards. The city came alive for just a few hours. Forgetting its charred past, it purified itself in the night.

Yet he was there in the morning. He was rooted, as always, to the same spot where he had been yesterday and where, no doubt, he would still be tomorrow. There he was, wearing his dirty boubou and his faded turban, sitting against a tree, a cane at his side. He had a haggard face and his hands were bony. He seemed to be dreaming. But what are the dreams of a jaded man made of?

Why had he chosen that spot? Was it because of the smell of warm bread wafting from the ovens or was it because of the smell of the white flour early in the morning?

He was homeless. He was there as he might have been anywhere else.

He remained in front of the bakery day and night, through the seasons. It did not matter whether it was the mango or orange season, whether flame trees blazed in their fiery splendour, or whether the grass turned brown like the straw used to make baskets. He was tired of waiting for some glance to be cast in his direction and for a hand to be held out towards him. The comings and goings of customers were no more than furtive images. The faces he saw remained unfamiliar and ordinary. He knew that at the end of the day there was no more to him than his mendicity.

But this was his territory and the red tinge from the dust on his boubou was the evidence. The customers at the bakery were his customers. They were his daily bread. Nothing in the world would move him from there.

Until, one day, the child arrived out of the blue. Nobody knew where he came from, but one day, he was there, rooted like a young mango tree.

In the beginning, he hung around the bakery watching people and playing alone in his corner. But, very soon, he drew nearer. The old man was oblivious to his presence until the day when they both ran towards the same customer.

Colliding into the child filled the old beggar with horror. He looked at the child from head to toe. A grave error had been committed. This profanation of his territory went well beyond reason.

He had to be there alone. That was clear. He knew no other way of being. He withdrew under a tree and set about meditating. Was it possible that a child could disturb his peace? He looked keenly at the boy. He weighed and analysed each gesture, and each coin that people gave him felt like a blow. He had to talk to him. He was sure the boy would go away.

But the child was imprisoned in profound silence. No sound

filtered into his ears. No words issued from his mouth. His world was plunged into an immobile stupor, into a deep abyss. For him, the gurgling of water and laughter did not exist. His eyes could record only mute images.

The boy was alone, the city like a carnival without music, a dance floor without a band.

Very soon, the old beggar was filled with exasperation by the presence of this other being. The situation deteriorated. Money grew scarce. Customers ignored him, preferring the outstretched hands of the young one. The hot air beat down on his face. He wiped his hot forehead. This heat, this heat. Was this wretchedness?

He went towards the child shouting threats. He performed menacing gestures, but the child did not understand the contortions of the old man's mouth, his rolling eyes and his face distorted by anger. Then, the old man hit him. The child retreated and fled. On the road, loud braking was heard, then nothing moved. The pedestrians waited for the shock. After the sound of braking would come the crash and then the thudding sound of a falling body. But that was not the child's destiny. The car stopped without touching him.

The old beggar thought for some time that his threats had worked but, the following day, there was the child. You could make out his silhouette against the shimmering sky. He stretched his hand to the bakery workers who gave him pieces of warm bread. He took them delicately, and then went and sat down in a corner to eat in small, slow, respectful bites. After he finished eating he would sketch strange patterns on the red soil.

The old beggar had now ceased all activity. He found getting up to beg and suffer a fresh rejection each time, pointless. It was obvious to him that he was of no interest to anyone.

He thought that he now had to take more drastic measures. He had to recover the peace he had known before, regain the feeling of satiation and the certainty that he could face tomorrows without dread.

Once his mind was made up, he waited until the sun had retired, leaving the city in a glow of red, orange and gold. At the hour when goats went back to sleep, when dogs came out of their kennels, when bicycle headlights came on, the rhythmic pace of the city could be heard humming everywhere.

At that hour when people slumber in oblivion and when stars twinkle with gold and mystery, the child slept, curled up in an empty cardboard box. The nearby shop had shut and he had stationed himself in the doorway.

The old man picked up a piece of wood and silently approached the sleeping form. Without looking, he hit him hard and fast. He struck him until he ran out of breath. The furious pounding of his heart made him throw away the big stick and flee.

Just as the cocks began to awaken the city with their crowing and cats stretched, a worker, setting out on his long morning walk, found the child's body. The deep wounds on his face were covered in blood.

It was the mango season. Fruits choking with juice were rotting under the trees. A strong stench filled the air. A dust-cloud drifted across the sky. The city was awakening. It must have been well past six o'clock.

Six

XIV

It is definitely a century that hangs its head in shame. Our elders have been called impotent, and we are accused of being 'limp' (although that is stretching the metaphor a little too far).

Someone replies to this: 'It is a matter of infrastructure and superstructure. The problem must be analysed in the specific context of the country. A lot of progress has been made. We are no longer the way we used to be.'

The young point their fingers at their 'Elder Brothers': 'What have you done to change things?' they ask.

Indeed, the town lost its scent a long time ago. We are all sick and tired of this suffocation, of this monarch lording it over his people. Everybody can feel that this is a sterile century. Even love is finding it hard to thrive.

XV

Now he is back after all this time. It should have been cause for celebration but I have nothing to offer. Walls encircle us. I think that we are going to suffocate.

This should have been a celebration. After all those days that trickled like drops of water, all those nights when I had lost all hope. Time had strayed from its abode in the abyss of my solitary room.

How often did I swear that he would come back!

It is as if I am still waiting for him, the void unfilled. His presence has not stirred the city. The neighbours have not said a word, any more than the cat has spared him a smile.

XVI

Today I dug the earth by hand and planted some seeds. To watch them grow. My fingers are wet and black. I heap the soil gently at first and then vigorously. A warm heat spreads through my body.

I went back to his room and touched his things: a pair of trousers on the bed, and an open suitcase. His clothes have changed. His perfume is different. But I still recognised his scent the way you remember having dreamed, the morning after a long night of sleep.

XVII

I want to pour libation and summon the gods, undo what has been done, utter sacred words to quell the fires, reduce to cinders promises made.

I want an assembly of diviners and sorcerers to chase away the evil spirits, to recapture the present once more.

I therefore call upon each and every one of you, djinns with hideous faces, juju-makers with terrifying powers. Come from all directions. I want to make peace. Escape through my pores, flee through my mouth and return to the earth.

I need the spell that will erase the memories.

XVIII

I must leave behind denials and errors. I will think of him with great lassitude. I will no longer know his whereabouts, or what has become of him. I will no longer know whether the memory has faded or whether his pain still persists.

I wanted to believe in fairy tales, believe I could journey on the back of a camel and spend my afternoons sipping tea.

Now, I have to start all over again.

XIX

His house was at the edge of the neighbourhood, at the end of a bougainvillaea-bordered alley. To get there, you had to walk past an Anago's shop and the women selling fried fish and attiéké. After that, you had to walk up a small hill passing an ochre-coloured church on the left and then continue down along the stony path.

She knew the way by heart. She had walked that way several times, straight from school when the daylight had not yet begun to fade and her absence had not as yet begun to worry anybody.

It was always the same: once inside, he would lock the door and undo her hair.

'You look like Mamy Wata,' he would whisper to her, 'you know, the water goddess. At nightfall, she comes from her queendom and seduces all the men she meets. Those who follow her are engulfed by the tides.'

He would then ask her to lie down and pull up her blue and white uniform. He would then lie next to her.

'Here, suck this sweet and then kiss me.'

In the darkness of the room, she forgot the world outside; the school, her friends, and the games they played. Yet she sometimes wondered whether he had lied the other day when he promised to change himself into a bird and fly to her when night fell. She had waited in her bedroom, in vain.

That afternoon it rained. You could hear the drops drumming on the roof like the repetitive notes of a xylophone. The air was dense. He asked her to take off all her clothes. When she was completely naked, he kissed her several times. He caressed her hair. Then he remained silent. Finally, he spoke in a low voice.

'I can't. You are too young.'

She raised herself on her elbows and jutted her head forward.

'Too young for what?' she yelled at him. 'For what?'

SEVEN

XX

Some people die without anyone even realising it. No drums, nor fanfare. You open the papers and see their faces:

Here is one with a half smile that makes him look shy. Then, there is the young woman with a radiant smile and shining eyes.

All of a sudden, there, in the middle of a page, a familiar face, someone you love:

The Divo family
The Commandant in Abidjan
The education adviser
The teacher in Daloa
The agricultural assistant in Bonoua
The Sassandra family
The Tabou family
announce with deep sorrow the death of their beloved brother, father, grandfather, nephew and brother-in-law. He passed away at the CHU of Cocody after a brief illness.

XXI

She stares at the photo that she has now hung on her wall. She sees his face, his reassuring smile creased with fine wrinkles returning her gaze, his short grey hair, and she tells herself that perhaps she had not loved him enough.

Where was she when he died? What was she doing at the time? She has no recollection. All she remembers was the first time when she heard the words that kill and alter the universe. The power of the word. If she had been out of town or if people had not told her, she would never have known that he had died. She would have thought that he was still in the big courtyard.

It is seven in the evening. The village is beginning to bustle. Her grandfather is looking at the women cooking rice in heavy pots. He thinks that tomorrow is Saturday and his son will be coming with his whole family. It will be just as it has always been. The big car will appear at the gate of the courtyard bringing with it city smells. There will be the children's joyous shrieks, hugs, and simple words.

The younger ones will bring chairs. Everyone will gather round. Somebody will stand up and say:

'Akwaba! How are things with you?'

XXII

The ghostly cortège that crosses your path makes the night scary.

Eyes blind and the body damp, you think that sleep is never going to come. Then, thoughts of regret flash through your mind, and those days wasted in too much wandering. And what of tomorrow, which has no rhyme nor reason and which is hazy and silent?

EIGHT

XXIII

Who are you?
You – who knocks at my door
On those dark moonless nights
That thrust through my sleep
And drain my blood
– In the morning –
My mind shatters into fragments
And all I want is to run, run, run
To the end of the road
The savannah's aflame
Bush fires are cursed
The city's dried of breath
By unrelenting harmattan
This being the season of

Desire

XXIV

I searched for such a long time. At the beginning, an image: an
ebony-warrior coming from Azania. Then it was like a three-
way mirror reflecting my past, present and future.

I searched for you everywhere: in my books, at the cinema,

within my weaknesses, under the fine folds of my smile.

Then, I lost faith. From one hurt to the next I kept running into loneliness and I said to myself, 'I will have a child on my own.'

At last, you surprised me from amidst a crowd.

XXV

From the silence of my heart I hear you breathe. Days are short and nights warm. Good fortune smiles upon me. You would think I had done her a favour.

Life unfurls like a red carpet and I frolic and dance, make faces at bad oracles, stick my tongue out at sceptics and dismiss the unbelievers.

My hours are drawn in arabesques, hyperbole and curves. My body fills with abundant joy.

I raise my arms to the sky and thank the gods for making me so fertile. I have given birth to hope.

XXVI

You changed my city. Painted her in a rainbow. I no longer recognise street names. Trees fleet by. The neighbourhoods are all different from each other, Yopougon, Cocody, Plateau, Macory. I charge at full speed down the secondary roads off the highway. Your plane leaves at five o'clock. We will get there on time.

XXVII

You fly to another place. Home, to a big city of stone.

You leave as one does. One always leaves. But you do not know if you will ever return. And it is always the same question that is repeated over and over again. 'I am leaving, I am leaving, will I ever return?'

I am leaving you today. Yesterday, I had already left you.

XXVIII

The grip tightens again and the circle shrinks. I feel unable to move any more.

Could it be your love that drains so much energy? This love which possesses me and makes me sever links? Come and join you ... Leave with you ... Is this not dying a little? Dying a fake death. Not the real death, but the sort that severs you from everything and covers the earth with a veil of solitude.

XXIX

It is absence that really kills me. That is what will finally be the death of me. I tell you, it will kill me. I should be used to it by now, but each day it grabs me by the neck, holds a knife against my throat and drains all my strength.

It is always others who die. They leave you there in the middle of life and you have no idea whether you dreamt it or whether time still exists. Absence makes me wary. A kind of interminable waiting suspended in the clouds.

And it is always the same thing. Each day that dawns wears

an ashen face, and each night that falls wears bloodshot eyes.

XXX

The fighter acknowledges his adversary. He will be his own opponent. Fear is what he must overcome. He never bows his head. He never allows anyone to kneel before him.

His humility is not the kind you find in beggars though. The leper licks the ground. The fighter has a proud heart. These are not my words. I read them somewhere.

NINE

XXXI

She has been writhing and battling with the pain for three days. The sheets, which had been changed, were already drenched in sweat. A soft light bathed the small room. The flowers had opened and some petals littered the small bedside table.

He looked at her and he knew that he loved her more than ever. He could hear her weak and regular breathing which echoed like a distant refrain. How long he remained like that looking at her suffering, he did not know. How long he was going to remain there like that, helpless, feeling her trickle away, he did not know.

He felt like screaming, so loud that the sound would pierce the walls, its reverberations would silence the city and time would recoil. He wanted to submit his body to the same suffering – feel this pain which now replaced pleasure.

Then, he prayed. He knelt down and prayed. He had not done this in a long time. There was an age when simple words lifted fear. Days when time was not of the essence. Now he was hesitant. He had a strong longing for his childhood prayers.

He placed his hands together, not so much to call to a god, but more to gather his strength. He stayed like this until evening. When the last sounds had been heard and the city seemed to be sleeping, he looked at her and found that she had woken up.

'I will go with you to death,' he said to her. 'I want to love you till the end of your suffering.'

'You cannot stop death,' she murmured. 'It is too strong. Do you remember Orpheus and Eurydice? What shall we do in this city, abandoned to despair and non-believers? You know it: the disease is devouring me.'

'I'll go to the end of our story.'

'Very well,' she said, and she fell asleep again.

Then he picked her up in his arms and walked through the city. He crossed deserted neighbourhoods. He walked above roads, above rooftops, through the green foliage of the trees. After travelling for several days and nights, he was exhausted. He placed her on some thick grass in a garden.

'Don't be afraid, I won't leave you. There is still a long way to go, but together, it should be easier. Drink some water, it will make you feel better.'

He gave her water, which she drank in small sips, and when she had finished, they continued on their way. She dozed in his arms. This time he crossed streams, small and large rivers, he hopped across swamps and ran on lakes.

They came to the sea. They marvelled at what they saw, and she said:

'I want to die here. What can be more beautiful than this dancing foam and engulfing water?'

'No, please, not yet,' he said and he listened to the waves which seemed to show him the way.

They travelled for seven more days as far as the white mountains. The silence and cold were one. The awesome void swallowed all vision.

'I could not die anywhere else. This is where peace lies. Just look at this immensity where no impurity can stain death. Even the soil rests beneath the cold. My body will retain its youth. The passing centuries count for nothing. Leave me here.'

'No,' he said, looking at her with compassion. 'This solitude chills my soul. I could never leave your body on this carpet of ice. I would feel as though I had betrayed you.'

He still had a long way to go on this painful journey. But then, before he came to the desert, they knew they had now reached the end of the earth and there was nowhere else for them to go. She looked him straight in the eyes:

'This is it. Now leave me. I must cross the desert gates alone. Beyond those are the souls of the dead. There is nothing more that you can do. Following me would be futile.'

His heart began to race. He suddenly felt that he was going to lose her.

'Let me love you one last time.'

And so it was there, between the earth and the sky, that they loved each other so intensely that the sun was eclipsed and a cool wind swept their bodies.

In the morning, she lay dead.

TEN

XXXII

The boy is like a human lizard. He drags his sluggish limbs across the city. He is always surrounded by a horde of snotty-nosed kids who run around him shrieking in all directions of the wind.

The town is deaf to his disability. A thick tension wraps itself around the buildings and nobody can escape the anxiety imposed by the days of drought. The air is filled with an acrid and obsessive smell.

The boy has become a thorn in the flesh of the young woman, a vision of her own wound, like a disease which ails her and which gnaws at her soul.

At the beginning she was able to quell her anxiety by giving him some coins, but she soon realised that this was not going to be enough. This truth dawned upon her the day that the boy disappeared. He was nowhere to be found, not even in his usual haunts, and nobody seemed to have any idea where he might be found. She wondered what might have happened to him, whether he had fallen ill or whether he had left the city.

For the inhabitants, nothing had changed. They continued in their daily comings and goings, performing rituals which ushered in the mornings and welcomed the nights. Walls kept their secrets and the streets colluded. Silence set. She slowly began to believe that she would never see him again.

Then one ordinary afternoon, as she bought fruit from a hawker, a child, completely out of breath, ran up to her and told her that the boy had been arrested and imprisoned. He asked for her help.

The building was at the end of the city. She had to walk up a rugged path to get there. It was a fair walk and they picked up plenty of dust on the way, so much so that they could no longer see their shoes. Then, finally, they began to make out the ugly, ochre walls of the building rising in the distance.

Inside the building, darkness reigned. A terrible stench rose from the flattened earth floor. You could hardly breathe crushed in the oppressive, clammy atmosphere. She asked to see the boy. The guard looked at her curiously, handed her a piece of paper to sign and then disappeared. After a few minutes, he reappeared accompanied by the boy.

She walked towards him. He half-raised himself with his left arm and shook her hand. Then he spoke very rapidly. He swore that he had not stolen the old woman's money, that he had never had any such intentions, and that the neighbours had wrongly accused him. 'You've got to get me out of here,' he said. 'Nobody has come to fetch me. If this goes on any longer, I will die.' The young woman listened. She could see the rash covering his skin, his distorted torso, and his legs, which were reddened by soil. She reached down towards him and offered him some biscuits and the cloth she had brought for him. 'I'll take care of you,' she replied.

The judge received her courteously. They had a brief meeting during which she learnt that there were no formal charges against the boy. She put up bail for him and managed to secure a commitment for his early release.

A few days afterwards, she ran into him while walking in town. He wore the cloth she had given him around his neck. When she came up to him, he supported himself against the wall and struggled to pull himself up using the strength in his elbows. She admired his courage. They talked like old friends.

The next day he came to her house at her request. Together they decided that he should sell cigarettes and sweets as a means of making a bit of money. She bought the wares at the super-market. They arranged them together in a wooden box.

For several days, the boy positioned himself opposite the pharmacy. He rediscovered his band of street children and spent hours under the huge baobab tree, waiting for prospective customers. It was a strange sight. Not many people were falling over themselves to buy cigarettes from a youth whose hands were the colour of dry soil. Nevertheless, his little business was not faring too badly. One day, he even brought his takings to the young woman for safekeeping.

One morning, however, he knocked on her door and when she opened it she found him in tears. Someone had relieved him of his box while he slept. He had nothing left. She consoled him. 'Don't worry. I'll get some more stock,' she told him, handing him a thousand-franc note. 'Come and see me in two days' time.' She watched him go.

First one week passed, then another without a word from the boy. Clouds were just beginning to gather in menacing clusters, and everyone waited for the downpour. She saw the beggars at the market gate and the city seemed to have forgotten everything.

It happened at around midday. She spotted the boy coming down the main shopping street in a wheelchair. It was not one of those shiny chrome ones you find in those special shops, but a brightly painted blue one made by a local metalworker.

The young woman was so surprised she stood rooted to the spot on the pavement.

She does not know why, but, from that day onwards, whenever the boy saw her, he distanced himself from her as quickly as possible. All this has gone on for such a long time now that they have fallen into the habit of just exchanging glances like two strangers in a city.

Eleven

XXXIII

I can hear a flute playing. The sound drifts from far away.

Yet he is here, nearby. I can see him in my mind. And the same air keeps on playing. It keeps playing. Incessantly. It stops me from thinking.

Last night I dreamt that I was kissing him. He was faceless but I knew it was him. When I woke up, it was late in the morning. I could hear his flute.

It all began with a smile. A way of speaking. Shoulders, neck, and that was it.

And I have this fear in the pit of my stomach and I tell myself that it has got to stop. That I had better leave, soon.

XXXIV

You must leave before you die, before the flame that ignites hope fades. Leave before indifference sets in, before too much is said and silence sealed. Leave while there is still time with your desire which conquers the sea. Powerful. The sea, nothing but the sea. Supreme and beautiful. An immense placenta, a liquid prison.

There will be no more tomorrow, but only the sea and sky paving themselves a passage across the horizon.

XXXV

In the beginning, it was strong. And then, after that, everything crumbled. Slowly the images fade and you tell yourself you would have given everything just to discover the scent of his body, discover that the blood coursing through your veins was made of molten lava. Your heart is no longer brimming and the desire has fled. No more of those nights filled with expectation. No more of those pleasurable sleepless nights.

Tomorrow, when you see his profile, things will have changed. Your glance will merely drift over his soul. You will feel neither remorse nor relief. You will only remember what his skin smelt like, and the strength of his neck. You will only remember his long fingers.

XXXVI

Your letter tells me that you love me. That you are waiting for me. Life is beautiful when we are together.

Your letter. Those words, written on the pages of a notepad. I would rather it was something other than paper. How quickly it crumples, how quickly it burns.

Enclosed is a photo. The colours are vibrant and the sea a turquoise blue. You can see the end of a boat. The wind caressing my face and your eyebrows knit against the glare of the sun. The sea and sky have the same festive air. It was so simple on the boat. The universe possessed us.

XXXVII

Increasingly, I feel myself slipping. There are days when I can hear myself speak; I can hear myself breathe.

Your letters are on my bedside table and I am no longer happy. You are far away. The sheets of paper tell me so. Such delicate paper, so fragile.

XXXVIII

I sleep into the middle of the afternoon. I feel restless. I drag my feet. Now that the rains are here, boredom has set in. The skies are furious. A gale rises and sheds its heavy load in huge drops. The city has lost its inhabitants who are curled up, grounded in their homes.

My feet get wet. I can hear the dreadful din of rain pelting the tin roof of the car. The headlights penetrate the sheet of rain. I watch nature bow down to drink in huge gulps.

XXXIX

The days breathe in reverse. Soon it will be time to depart. The flight is only in one week's time. You are waiting for me.

I no longer know how to live these days that flash by. The relentless drumming of my heart seems to be ripping my arteries apart. The night is a vast lagoon.

I am wearing myself down. I can feel it. I am covered in a rash from all this anxiety. An urge to go, to stay. A desire to love just you alone, and yet not leave everybody behind, saps my strength.

I would like to walk to the limit, then lie down gently on the ground. I just want to sleep. Sleep, and have organza dreams. Sleep, until evening curls up allowing the sounds of nature to pause. Sleep, until my breath lulls me to sleep.

Waiting. This is what is wearing me out. These days have minds of their own. Your letters fill me with longing.

XL

Days fizzle and I let the hours drain away. Today, waiting fills me with joy. Nothing out of the ordinary. I just want time to drown so that I can be left in peace.

You will understand, my friends, if I leave you now, it is to go far away, in order to come closer. Overcome silences.

Yesterday, while walking in a field, I saw a snake, my feet only a few centimetres away from its velvety head. It was coiled around itself and gazing at me. There was no menace in its eyes, no fear. I was deeply moved by the beauty of this creature warming itself in the morning sun. I could just as easily have been some wild grass or a handful of earth, or even a running stream.

You will understand that there is plenty of hope where I am going. I will have a lot of things to give and a lot to recount.

I must leave so as to return forever, knowing that nowhere else can the soul exist, and nowhere else can encounters be more wonderful or promises greater.

XLI

Such a great sorrow, such a never-ending story, days lamented yesterday and today. She counted sheep at night and could not lay her insomnia to sleep. Retracing her steps might have healed her pain, but there were enough roads leading to purgatory. People stared at her and she had no idea what to say to them. She could have gone where she was supposed to, but the memory of all of you always followed her.

What to do? She took charge of those tough years and savoured the delight of the dew at dawn. She accepted the regrets and remorse and, owing to a gesture she no longer anticipated, something stirred in the depth of her soul.

Her mouth looked less pretty in the marbled mirror. The small creases layered like numerous faded flowers, and what of the woman she dreamt of becoming? Should she continue believing in the dream, or just give up?

Doubts and still more doubts nag and niggle, ceaselessly. So strong and persistent in the pit of her stomach, at breakfast, and all day long.

She wanted to remain curled up without moving. Waiting. Without moving. Listening to the seasons exhale. Watching the sun's birth in the middle of the sky.

The pounding cannons have ceased. The sound of machine guns has stopped, and people pick up the dead. Only the low sound of a final groan can be heard rattling the silence in the battlefield. Fear starts to lift and hope returns. The tension in the muscles begins to ease.

You can feel a breeze blowing. All is not in vain.

TWELVE

XLII

Somewhere, a young man wallows in his suffering – his wound so deep he cannot draw a distinction between love and destruction. When he fights, he wounds his adversary like a fighter in search of victory.

He fades into a wilderness. The city withdraws from him as he watches life drift away.

His pain is so great that he wants to punish all women, but I tell him, 'No, love is the colour of hope. Bitter today, sweet tomorrow. You should not throw away your wealth of tenderness and let the honey-filled caresses dry up. Do not be wicked just to prove who you are, just to expose your wounds to the skies.'

Love is a story that we never stop telling. Let yourself be lulled by its sweet words. Adorn yourself with its multiple charms but please, do not spoil your life. True love, excuses in the name of love, sacrifices, disappointments. You must survive.

I have seen many women curled up, licking their wounds, muttering, suffering headaches, their minds elsewhere. I have seen many women collapse.

I want a sexy woman with a strong and steady voice. Love you through tenderness to melting point. I want to undress you and give you all that I have. If this should give you reason to sting my soul and to cuff my wrists, then, at that point, I shall leave you.

I do not understand those men who want to tear women up and kick them in the gut with evil words that hurt to the depths of the soul.

They ought to be told to stop, held at bay and taught the alphabet from scratch.

But let us forget all that and let me tell you something else:

XLIII

It is about this guy selling an umbrella in the rain.

He holds it firmly against himself. His shirt is drenched and his face is soaked. His trousers cling to his legs. His feet swim in the muddy water. He keeps the umbrella in a plastic sheath and he looks nervously for a buyer.

He is one of those many characters you find hanging around on the streets. Not poor enough to get you worried. Neither a hunchback, nor lacking an arm. He is just the sort that you do not even notice. This could have happened in your city or mine.

THIRTEEN

XLIV

Here, in this flat thousands of kilometres away from you all, I feel a light filter through my heart. Through the window I see trees swaying. Some children are playing in the park and screeching like cockatoos.

After all, I have never left you.

In the mornings you get up and go to work. I am alone all day long. In a short while, I am going out to catch a breath of fresh air, or maybe I will even read a book.

We need some coffee and some milk. We still have some butter.

XLV

In the heart of this big city of stone, the sun sheds a different sort of light and it remains lukewarm. It seems that words have double meanings and that people walk on cushions of air.

Yesterday I was at home. Today I am here. I wait for you but you are nearby. I wait for you and we walk down the street.

But I sometimes wonder why I am here. So far away from home. This love took me by the hand, brought me to a country which means nothing to me.

It is grey outside. I get up when it rains and listen to the sound of a jackhammer in a nearby building site. Under the duvet, I shiver from the cold although the window is closed. Some classical music plays on the radio.

Wake. Wash. That feels a lot better. The water touches my skin. The feeling of the air filling my lungs. Then in a flash, time begins to fly.

XLVI

I need to feel the heat and sweat running down my back, feel warm nights humming with insects, the dust and the mud. At home, life sprouts everywhere. You have nowhere to hide. You can never forget that there is still much to be done.

XLVII

The weather is dull again. This is a bad summer. My heart skips a beat. I saw a fox through the window of the train taking us to the countryside. A red fox. He had two feet up against a slope peering into a poultry-yard.

I do not know what is happening to us. Nothing seems to work and everything seems so tough. Our love is slipping away.

Life is a trap. I am going crazy in this city that revolves around you, where my life has taken on the allure of a promise. I am suffocating. Love brought me here and has left me comatose until daybreak.

XLVIII

His mother has a huge cancerous growth the size of a fist in the middle of her bloated belly. The growth gets larger, destroying her cells.

She looks exhausted, shrivelled up in her wicker chair placed by the window. She can see the garden and the trees with their leaves rustling gently. A cool breeze filters into the room and flutters the curtains like the wings of a morning butterfly. Voices mumble on the television projecting furtive images. She looks through her window to the path leading up to the road and she can see flashes of her life in black and white.

It is too late now, even though her son has returned after all these years of silence. She knows only too well that he thinks she is going to die. If this were not the case, why would he be here now when this rot has taken root in the depths of her body? He looks at her and tries to be kind. He says innocuous things to her which would make her believe that she still has a son.

She has never understood why he left. She does not know why he comes to see her every day. She wonders whether she is pleased to see her son. His presence seems to weigh down heavily on her. She does not know what to tell him. She can no longer find the words. She had stopped waiting for him.

She remembers all their quarrels and all the things he shouted to her face: 'You are mad! Mad!' Of course she was mad! She has known it for years. Was it her fault if her life was a failure, that things had never worked out as she had planned? She loved her husband. She loved him enough to want to die when he left with another woman. She remembered the hurt and the shame, the shame, the shame.

She looks exhausted, shrivelled in her wicker chair placed by the window.

He tells his friends that he does not care whether she dies

or not. He has never really loved her. He left home when he was barely fifteen, and in any case, he felt more at home at the neighbours'. They were the ones who mattered.

You can tell by the way he speaks of his mother that he feels a lot of resentment towards her. He says that she used to have an endless stream of hysterical crises. He also says that she used to be possessive. But he had now made up his mind to no longer think of all those things.

The young woman he had been living with for five years has left. When he returned from a trip she announced that it was all over between them. So he locked himself up in his flat. He cried, suffered insomnia, migraines. Then, one morning, he went to see his mother.

He does not really want anything from the old woman. But he feels that he can help her.

He sees himself holding her hand. He will wipe her brow. Whisper soothing words to her. Listen to her sleep. His mother is dying and he wants to be there.

FOURTEEN

XLIX

In the hotel where we are staying there is a woman who is unfaithful to her husband. She is very beautiful. Her hair is short and blonde and she has a tan.

The first time I saw her on the beach, I did not recognise her until she raised her head and smiled at us. I remember it was a dark green day and the sand was boiling hot. The water was invigorating. When you dived, head first, intense cold gripped you. Pores sealed immediately. The cells pressed against each other. The body became smooth, covered in scales.

The earth disappears under the water. Body submerged, it feels like the beginning of time. You have an urge to remain there. Sounds filter through the skin, light penetrates you and thousands of small bubbles erupt.

She swims with her eyes closed. Salt in her mouth. Waves carry her, toss her up and down, pick her up again, engulf her and then let go of her again.

How the sun shines as never before! The sea delivers her as if she were being born in the middle of the day. She is happy with this love that takes her breath away. Soon the sky will have swept away the glistening, mirror droplets.

When the sun shines, all is well. It burns the skin with a fire of truth and the soul tiptoes away.

The sand sketches endless castles on the sea, reawakening childhood. In the distance, you can hear the sound of unfathomable words. Your body warm and wet.

The sun is far too hot, the water a deep, deep blue. The horizon seems to be etched in colour pencils.

When the sun is here, all is well. Wounds heal and the heart grows tender. The wind is there to sing your story. It whispers whatever you want it to. Time takes a break. With the sun here, all is well.

Every afternoon, a man joins her on the sand and together they play a game of lovers. They lie in each other's arms looking sensuously at each other and caressing each other suggestively. They are almost making love. You can feel that she yearns for his desire and that in the end, she will determine their destiny. They look like strangers who have only just met, owing to the sunshine on an island renowned for its beauty.

When the stinging heat subsides a little and the sky begins to cool down, they part.

She walks alone on the path leading to the hotel, perched on the rocks and decorated with local stones. She walks up the steps to her room and opens the door. There, she finds her husband.

In the evening when couples take a walk in the warm evening air and marvel at the splendour of the reddening sunset, she looks like any other woman in love, walking beside her chosen one.

L

The ancient ember-coloured city was beautiful and its roads looked as if they had never changed. One could hear the sighs of the centuries as they settled in many successive fine layers. You held my hand and showed me the red bricks, the wonderful statues. Clear water from the fountains sprayed an inner music in the air.

The narrow streets tried to capture the light over and over

again. A sea sky. I would have loved to lie down on the ground in this eternal city, which feeds off fresh ruins.

LI

It always comes as a shock. First, doubt, followed by anger. An urge to hit somebody, break their bones to pieces; annihilate a sick mind who, in broad daylight in this marvellous city, reawakened a deep wound in me.

This hand, suddenly, so close to my body, to my person. This unknown hand. A filthy hand that sullies, quick, while boarding a bus in the jostling crowd.

And so the world crumbles, and beauty vanishes faster than it came, leaving a stain on the city.

There, from deep in the recesses of my mind, a memory resurfaces – this time, even more unclean – from a long time ago.

A hand in a half-lit cinema, a hand whose intention I could not fathom. It grabbed mine. Urgent. The music. The film. Voices. The dark. A moist penis. The man running away. An irreparable sensation.

FIFTEEN

LII

Here we are now, back in this big city of stone, which has turned cold. The evenings fall rapidly. It is only four in the afternoon but already dark. The street lamps light up strangely. It is terrible, this endless obscurity. It takes you by surprise, just when you thought you still had time. It feels like a betrayal. A compulsory rest imposed upon you despite your insomnia.

We have become little grey creatures. Rounded shoulders and round bellies. I cart my misery around, not knowing what is causing my voice to tremble and my soul to drown. For days now, I feel trapped, pacing about in my cage, my throat tightly constricted. What is happening to me? I am drained of all energy, and the beat of my heart has altered to an unusual rhythm. Under these covers, still warm from the heat of the night, I find myself suffocating. What is happening to me in this odourless city?

LIII

Here there are no griots, only poets. You think that you are leading an extraordinary life and that people see you as you would like them to. You adorn yourself with your writing. It becomes your identity, your bread and butter, and your reason for living. You begin to believe in what people say. You become locked up in your creation, become submerged in words, and sentences suffocate you in the solitude of your retreat. They make you forget the blood and the dust.

LIV

I think of my country, far away, and my eyes open beyond space.

In this vast city, words travel fast. I am bombarded with ideas. I see myself in that large conference room, listening keenly to writers from Africa – Angola, Ghana, Uganda, Kenya, Nigeria ... One of the speakers proclaims:

'It is our duty to understand our place in the history of humanity. An African literature cannot exist until the day we liberate ourselves from the arrogant criticism of the West.'

LV

I dream of my country, which obsesses me all the time. I carry it with me all day. At night, it lies next to me, making love with me.

LVI

We must stamp out bad habits, uproot false theories. We must face ourselves squarely. Time flies, it has nothing to lose. The seeds we sowed have now taken root. I think of Adjamé, Treicheville, Yopougon. I think of the three-lane motorway, lit in the dark humid night of an all too well-known village.

LVII

I think of Abidjan's gangsters, Bouaké's thieves, of the organised gangs of Korhogo. And I say, 'Just open your eyes! Open your eyes!' I say, 'Look at the sky. Its dark clouds herald a storm. The torrential rains will come with the sound of machine guns, and the roll of drums will come with the sound of military boots.'

I speak of Cocody, where the air is cool, where flowers bloom faster than in our pathetic neighbourhoods. I speak of the inequalities that breed like geckos under the ruins of slums.

LVIII

There is no reason for being forgetful. No justification for laughing with your arms folded across your chest. The lunatic's hair is tangled. The lice infesting his head are bloated with blood. The man stinks. His stench permeates the city.

LIX

I say, 'Be wary of your lucky star. It will fall from the heavens and become reduced to cinders and ash. It will cake into clay.'

I say, 'Be wary of those cheques with lots of noughts, those big-bellied bank accounts, and black lacquered Mercedes.'

Your gardens will be trampled upon, your sacred altars under siege, and your fetish idols beheaded. Your houses will crumble. Your books will be strewn on the ground, and your famous thinkers condemned. All traces of your footsteps will be erased and your chests will be pierced with poisoned arrows on abandoned beaches.

All this news will be broadcast live on television and radio, by satellite, telex and telephone. The whole world will be able to see your contorted mouths, the thick oozing blood and your gruesome bodies in their final last throes.

LX

Must you be blind, to not see?
Deaf, to not hear?
Mute, to not scream?

LXI

You want to believe in fairy tales and legends. Pray that things remain the same.

But really, it is obvious that the grass is not all that green, and the cows are not all that fat. If you stand back and think about it properly, you will realise that something has turned sour. You can no longer walk in the streets without thinking that something is not right. Times have changed. Admit it. Would you drink water from that lagoon?

LXII

We must perform cleansing rites. Make the necessary sacrifices. We must replant our great trees that have been uprooted, replenish our sacred forests that have been decimated.

Particles of wind were singing and, as at the time of the primal whirlwind, leaves were blown upwards into the sky. The word was complete. That word which is at once uttered and silent, both active and inactive. The one possessed only by the initiated.

The gush of wind. Growling from the steel in the heavens. The rain will be dry and hard. There will be nowhere to shelter. You will have to offer your face and uncover your head. The rite will take place in the heart of the city and across the land. Debris will hurtle down the corridors of power.

Sixteen

LXIII

One day, a woman and a man who were deeply in love decided to have a child.

'We cannot live like this without giving of our own blood,' said the woman. 'I would like to turn our love into living flesh.'

'The child will be a precursor of hope, I'm sure,' agreed the man, nodding his head. 'We will teach him all that we know.'

On the following day the woman was pregnant. Before the end of the day, she had given birth to a boy.

Then the man cried out:

'Love has triumphed! We have created life! Our son will be our messenger.'

Both father and mother remained close to the child and taught him to love and have faith. They constantly spoke to him. The child listened.

'You will travel through continents, and meet people. Tell them what we have taught you. Rebuild the cities destroyed by violence and oppression. Allow wild plants to grow and do not crush the clouds. Tell them of the water that never dries up. Dip your hand in the soil and inhale its scent, and above all, believe in yourself.'

When the child was ready, he bade his parents farewell without looking back. After a while, when there was sufficient distance between them, you could tell that he had grown. By the time he approached the sprawling city, he had already become a man.

Things were not easy. Wherever he went, all he saw was despair. Indeed, the city dazzled with bright lights and shimmered with wonders but just one false move would lead to mud and filth. Although people wore gold, if you just turned your head you would see the poor in tatters and the street children. If you came off the brightly lit streets and ventured further out, you would find yourself choking on the dust of abandoned tracks. All this was nothing, though. The worst part of it was that the inhabitants had lost hope. Some spoke of freedom and change but this was mere empty rhetoric. Nobody believed in it. The harmattan would blow for weeks and dry their skin, but the heat only continued to beat down harder after that and the stench worsened. People dragged themselves along, breathless.

What about him? What was he doing?

He spent his time growing. He looked at life, recorded everything with his eyes. He felt terribly exiled from the others. Communicating with them was so difficult that it became tortuous. What he was looking for seemed to be somewhere else. Sometimes he had an urge to leave, abandon the city in search of something else.

Moreover, he felt that he had changed. Well, not that much, but enough to recognise the difference within himself. He had to make a real effort to continue believing, and although it was true that he could still see his parents in his dreams and hear their gentle words, it was equally true that nightmares left him out of breath in the depth of night. He thought he was falling. His head reeled and he was frightened. He knew only too well that this was caused by anxiety. It was so thick and true he could have held it in his hands.

Anxiety was responsible for his unmaking. It was destroying his spirit and draining his strength. 'This has got to stop,' he decided. 'This has to end.'

At about that time he fell in love.

Her eyes were shaped like cowries and her skin was the colour of sand. You could see the city in her gaze.

For her, time was not an obstacle because she considered herself to be without gender. She was a creature in between, ambiguous, who could not care less if she wore a skirt or if she had pointed breasts.

For her, life flowed in regular tides and she knew how to make the most of it. She just got on with it. For her, love was an afterthought, like a fly in the ointment. She believed that she had many things to do. Her innocence draped her in an incomparable elegance.

Was this the reason why she was beautiful? The reason why he wanted to possess her? He was not quite sure. All he had was an insatiable desire. Morning and night, her scent stayed with him. For him it was a constant struggle; should he negate this persistent passion, or should he succumb to it?

She agreed to speak to him. She felt in him a strange strength although she was entirely oblivious of its meaning. She hung around listening to him and twisted around her finger the white handkerchief that her parents had given her. She knew that what he said was part of life but she was not ready for it. She needed some more time. Plenty of time, years maybe.

One evening she drank from the glass that he proffered. All of a sudden the light crashed. She felt drowsy. Her eyelids closed.

And so it was thus that he possessed her. In the city, people became petrified. A profound silence settled on the night. The light waned.

When she regained consciousness she was carrying a child in her womb.

'I'm dying,' she murmured. 'This child is not mine. It will bring misfortune.'

Then he realised the enormity of his betrayal, and panic seized him. He wanted to erase what he had done. Deny it. But her belly was as round as the globe. He placed his hand on her distended belly to check if the child was still alive.

Suddenly, a huge flash of lightning disturbed the clouds. The sky began to flee and the trees to howl. At the same time an infernal heat descended. A dense and dusty smoke encircled nature and set it aflame. A violent, hot torrent of air scorched people and overturned buildings. The skin peeled in layers. Eyes dried out. Hair fell in tufts. Everybody died violently. Metal began to melt and trail along the ground. The outline of a gigantic mushroom cloud framed the blazing horizon.

Seventeen

LXIV

He was a magician of acclaimed strength and powerful beauty. His knowledge of secrets knew no bounds.

People came from far and wide to see him. Some travelled the length and breadth of the globe to come. Others travelled on rugged, narrow paths. They all arrived full of hope and their heads full of desires. They waited anxiously for the chance to speak to him and ask him the impossible because they said that he possessed the secret formula for eternal happiness.

'Is the key to happiness not love, wealth or power?' they all asked him.

But the magician explained to those who could hear:

'Happiness is to be found in its absence. Can you walk with your eyes closed? Could you sleep eternally? Can you know silence?'

After hearing his words, many left. Their thoughts were heavy and their throats constricted. They did not understand what the magician meant. They returned to their lands and declared that the man had no power.

However, some decided to stay. They desperately wanted to decipher his secret. They were convinced that something lay hidden behind his words and nothing in the world was going to make them abandon their quest.

Maybe these were the more desperate ones because they were totally dependent on the magician. If he raised his arm, they immediately applied themselves to analysing the meaning of his gesture. If he scratched his head, coughed or yawned or cracked the joints of his knuckles, they rushed to take notes. The more gifted ones amongst them sketched diagrams, depicting his exact position at each precise moment. Conferences and debates were held.

The girl arrived during an evening debate. The master had already gone to lie down after having yawned profusely. The disciples sat in a circle discussing the significance of his yawns.

'The master yawned twenty times.'

'No! He yawned twenty-one times, I counted!'

A commotion ensued and a new debate began.

Now this girl hailed from a family of magicians. Her father was a magician and her mother had powers of the initiated. She observed, listened to each of them and decided to take a chance.

She sat on the floor with her legs crossed and gathered her vital energies. She shut her eyes. When she felt ready, she looked straight ahead of her. The magician was there, observing her. She waited. He held out his hand.

'What do you want? Why have you come here?'

'I'm not quite sure yet. I feel greatly troubled.'

'But you look happy. Your face is radiant and your energy is attracting others. If you fail you will lose all that you possess.'

'I would like to try. I do not know the nature of my joy. It comes and goes. Nothing seems to remain static. Everything is shifting and I am carried in a storm. I can no longer tell the difference between dreams and reality.'

There was a moment of silence. Then the magician smiled at her and said:

'I understand. Follow me and don't ask any questions.'

They entered a labyrinth with a glass wall. She could see everything that was happening on the outside, but she knew that she would never be able to find her way back again.

Finally, they came to a room draped with thick curtains.

She wondered whether there were any windows behind them. A great peace reigned in the complete bareness of the room. No unnecessary objects. No ornaments.

The magician came towards her, placed his arms around her neck and kissed her.

Later, she ran her fingers on the naked skin of the man with whom she had made love. He made love in a way that only sorcerers could. She caressed his neck, the arch of his back and his thighs. She could feel each cell, each atom. He slept in silence.

Detaching herself from him, she placed her two hands on his forehead and opened his skull.

She was petrified by what she saw inside, a desert of sadness and solitude. It looked like a battleground: trenches, barbed wire, craters. The ground was littered with corpses.

Just as she was about to flee, escape from the place of desolation, she spotted a lake in the distance, and a happy green meadow. The soil was fertile.

She shut his skull and slept next to him.

From that moment on, she spent the days trying to find a way of getting to the vast meadow stretched across the horizon. She dreamt of how she would roll on the grass and inhale the strong scent of the wet soil. Touching the warm earth, the reassuring earth, became her sole obsession.

She stayed by the magician's side night and day. To stop him from yawning all the time she told him stories that she made up on the spot. She loved it when she succeeded in making him burst into throaty laughter, and when he flung back his head, she was able to see his bare and vulnerable neck. What she feared most were those deafening silences that rebounded like the sound of wild galloping buffaloes.

When night fell, she entered his head again. She watched him sleep, and when she saw his body rise and fall gently, she knew that the moment had come. Indeed, she had prepared herself for the final voyage with utmost care. The battlefield was dangerous.

She broke an egg, washed her face three times and approached the sleeping man. Placing her two hands on his forehead, she opened his skull.

She walked cautiously but ripped her dress under barbed wire. She injured her leg in a trap. However, all that seemed like nothing as she successfully negotiated the buried mines and also managed to keep breathing despite the stench of putrefying corpses.

She came to the lake at last. She was hot and thirsty. She sat on the bank and drank some clean and cool water. A gentle breeze was blowing. On the other side, the meadow stretched endlessly.

After regaining her strength, she took a deep breath and plunged. On the bed, the magician stirred. He tossed and turned several times. Suddenly his eyes flew open and after looking around him, he leaped out of the sheets. The girl had disappeared. He yelled out her name at the entrance of the labyrinth.

The girl felt herself being sucked towards the bottom of the lake by a force beyond her. She sank. Water filled her mouth, her ears, and her nose. She could see algae performing their dance. She could not yell. All that she could think of was the shore.

Eighteen

LXV

I know this disease well. It gnaws at me and makes me sick with worry. It has brought me to a halt.

Autumn is such a beautiful season! The atmosphere captures the rust-coloured, dead leaves. The earth seems to bare her own nudity, her skin bedecked with a humid scent. It rains. There are changes in the skies. You can tell that something is going on.

LXVI

I can feel this disease which makes my head spin in the sunshine or under the steel clouds of this big city of stone. Does a world exist where the will to forget is not feigned?

Three times now, I have been unfaithful to you. Three, the evil number which makes the wind turn back on itself. Three times, I took the opposite path, walked backwards, and looked through the back of my neck.

LXVII

Three, the odd number which shatters my dreams. Unforgiving. Accuser. Who will be able to defend me now apart from the unbelievers, this crowd of shadowy figures who roam about the streets? Those who know neither North nor South and who preach abandon.

Who will be able to defend me if not the cynics, those creatures with metallic laughter that makes their bodies jerk disgracefully?

LXVIII

Room 465; fourth floor, on the left, at the end of the corridor. Here we are together. I start to tremble. I wrap myself in his smell, wet my face in his sweat, touch his skin, bite his shoulder, swallow his desire, close my eyes, arch my body; move up and down. This love which makes me lose my head feels like despair, like pleasure mingled with tears.

LXIX

I remember. A day like no other. The air was mild. I had not eaten breakfast; just had a cup of coffee and my belly was empty.

I remember. His scent filled my nostrils. His sweat made my mouth salty. I lapped up his force and energy, and discovered how famished my desire was.

His skin was taut like a painter's first canvas. His skin, the same colour as mine and above all, his sweat, oiling my belly, flooding the palms of my hands.

LXX

I left while he still slept in that hotel room which had become
ours. I closed the door gently. I took the lift, and found myself
on the street. The air was sharp, the light dim. I buttoned my
coat. My throat was tight.

I remember. Christmas was already in shop windows, and
the city flaunted its lights in the street. I started to think of
tomorrow, of times to come. There was something unreal yet
familiar. I said to myself, 'I hope the beauty lasts.'

LXXI

When a man gives so much of his strength and soul that the
woman is filled with awe by this deed, then beauty will have
knelt and paid tribute to the couple lying down in the dimly lit
room.

Is it possible to allow bodies to speak, to let them speak their
own language that transcends the frontiers of silence? How
would he have ever experienced such desire if deep down, the
nerves that carried love had never existed?

LXXII

It should have snowed but instead a clear sun shines, caressing
the big city of stone. It lends it a magical air, as if its inhabitants had power over the sky.

LXXIII

These stories are all very well, but not convincing. If the general belief is that one should behave, there ought to be a good reason for it. When everybody agrees that you ought not to play with the devil, there must be some grain of truth in it. The weather changes so quickly. If it suddenly turns cold, I would not be properly covered. There is no smoke without fire; if you find ashes, it must be that something has burnt.

LXXIV

Where does his desire come from? Where does it meet mine? I dreamt of a white horse with a red underbelly. A panther placed its paw on my shoulder. 'Yo', the word that invokes the primal silence.

NINETEEN

LXXV

On that day, my horoscope read, 'For some reason or other, it looks as if there will be many tensions in your love life this month. You feel uncertain about the future. But whatever the reason, everything will work out in due course, and you will look back to this period as a bad chapter in your life.' This happened at the time when many Indians died during the Carbide Union incident, a time when I saw I burnt corpses stretched out next to each other, their eyes blinded. The crying children had been exposed to toxic gas I that had escaped from the factory. These images reminded me of the emaciated bodies of the dying in Ethiopia, of the children with distended bellies that looked like carnival balloons. A little girl who refused to eat because her body had forgotten how to.

Indira Gandhi's corpse in flames. Reagan's re-election. The miners' strike, the hijack by Kuwaiti terrorists and the plane stranded on the runway. Fear inside. The killed hostages.

Then, that story in *Fraternite-Matin*: a woman goes to buy fish. The fish harbour. The thieves. The money box. A fleeing shop attendant. Suddenly, anger and panic. A bullet in the neck of the woman lying face-down. Woman from Abobo or Treicheville. Market woman with a loud voice. A fishmonger.

LXXVI

Sometimes, love is meaningless. Anger. Pity. The torment of answering questions.

Love sometimes burns hotter than a branding iron. It can destroy and deface the earth.

LXXVII

This has opened a wound that I thought had healed. Was it not folly to believe that things remained unchanged, that I would recover from the disease with time, and regain my balance? Yes, he might be right in cloaking himself in unparalleled silence. His refusal to accept life with all its ups and downs, where time erodes desires and maggots abound.

I want to write about him until I am purged of him. Utter his name to saturation point. Wrench him from my body and fling him onto the ground. Why do I go to him like the sea dissipating into foam?

I do not understand this story that crosses my life diagonally, poisoning my existence and leading me towards hell. I do not understand this musty story.

LXXVIII

We spoke of conquest. We spoke of destruction. We spoke of boredom. And he told me how he was finding life painful, of his interminable languor, and of his feeling of insatiable emptiness. As I looked at him the ground opened beneath my feet and I felt my spirit disintegrating.

The lassitude that fills his soul and makes him see the world askew, where does it come from?

Elsewhere, I might have tried to do something about it, but I am far from my source of strength. I no longer have the courage for those long battles that mutilate my soul. His wound is too deep. His dormant passion threatens my being.

LXXIX

It was madness to believe that bodies could banish loneliness, that pleasure could give birth to a fertile language.

LXXX

She wants to remember everything since the present is too strong and makes her head spin. All she trusts is her memory. Today could be an illusion. It hurts to live from one moment to the next.

She must remember so as not to feel the emptiness. She looks for some shreds of the past. Memory will lead her to tomorrow and beyond. The present is far too short. It is only meant to knit together the hours.

She remembers the words she uttered with a sob in her throat. 'You betrayed me.' He looked at her and replied, 'Betrayal, that is another matter.'

She remembered his departure. The aeroplane taking off on a humid night. Then she had driven off, gently, slowly, to the house. Directly. Hardly any red lights to stop her. She simply kept her hands on the steering wheel, changing gear with her eyes fixed straight ahead.

He returned later on of course, but they never broached the

subject again.

She feels somewhat like an animal. She lives by her instincts and can feel what others are only capable of thinking.

She exists by desire although she can feel it leaving her. It seems that their urges are different, that their instincts no longer coincide. Sometimes she wants him, but the moment is not right. At other times he wants her, but her mind is on other things.

She knows that there will be other nights; in fact, many other nights. They do not need to arrange a date. She falls asleep beside him.

Her condition worries her. She no longer feels anything. Her thoughts become elusive. She feels dazed. She loses things. She breaks glasses.

This is not normal. She wonders whether she has not invented it all, whether or not she has gone mad. A dangerous game, a mortal knowledge. Juggling with her mind is like playing with fire, the same as taunting the gods who have nothing to do with it.

Yet she is in one of those moods again which she cannot control. She watches the world through the window. She feels removed, whatever she does. There is nothing she can do about it. She has to let it pass. She knows how futile her efforts are. Animated conversation, calculated smiles and then SNAP! – she loses it.

She feels helpless, imprisoned in this closed space. She knows that she is looking at the void at her feet. She knows that she ought not to, that there are many other reasons for leaving, that it is coming from her mind not her body.

Why not share? Belong? There is no shortage of struggles. There is no shortage of good causes!

I could have given her a name but she has too many faces. I am sure that she is somewhere. I have seen her, met her. She has even been my friend. I remember. The only thing is, as in those cheap love storybooks, a man came between us. Oh, not for long! But long enough to make me let go of her hand. I recognised her in that woman who lives alone. She inserts her key in the lock. Opens the door. The cat miaows. I have also discovered her through this waitress in a nightclub, bathed in neon lights. I have seen her on television, announcing her suicide mission. A young Lebanese woman opposing Israeli troops.

I know her well, and would have named her but for her many faces.

TWENTY

LXXXI

She took the telephone off the hook and stared at the handset for ages before dialling the number.

'It is silly,' she thought as she listened to the phone ringing in the distance. Once ... twice ... before the third ring, she hung up. A shiver ran up and down her spine. She lay on the bed and shut her eyes. 'This is silly,' she thought as the phrase bounced in her head like a ping-pong ball.

Not a word from him. Nothing. It is several months now. From one day to the next.

She no longer recognises herself. She knows that this city is making her mad. At home, she would have reacted differently.

Outside, she is perspiring under her coat. She dislikes her odour, trapped within it. The wind hits her face continuously. Her skin becomes dry. She runs her hand through her hair which feels like cotton wool.

'It does not matter, I'll forget him. After all, this city is beautiful, with all its great stone buildings and its terraced houses. Walking in the park, feeding the ducks and buying hot chestnuts will suffice. What I need to do is work hard.'

'This is silly,' she told herself, and reached for the receiver again. It was cold, as cold as this draughty room. She waited a couple of minutes and then everything happened. The number, the voice at the other end of the line, and her own voice, clear and audible:

'Have you heard from him?'

LXXXII

The big city of stone is covered in a foggy veil. From my window, I can see skeletal trees dancing, swaying like a silent sea. He is gone.

LXXXIII

I have almost forgotten his face already. A host of other gazes intermingle, are mixed with his. I have even forgotten the sound of his voice. And here I am, bereft of all my belongings. All that remains is my writing. Words on a white sheet of paper. They whisper memories in my ear. They whisper inscribed words into my soul.

LXXXIV

I have turned him into a poet-genius, a fantastic mind. I built his silences into golden mountains, erected his words into triumphal arches.

An intense yearning rises from deep within me. I wanted to create some drama out of simple words. I made up what followed from anonymous gestures.

Now, I have to struggle against becoming embittered and command my soul to cease being sad.

There is no law. No judge. In the wilderness of the heart, you sometimes lose blood.

LXXXV

I rearrange the puzzle, move moments, recover memories. You live your life, and I live mine. There are a thousand stories, a thousand seasons of the heart.

I cannot see very far but I can hear what is being said. I am here dreaming away while others die in many terrifying ways.

I juxtapose destinies, record feelings. A soldier shoots the enemy and thinks of his loved one. He recollects their first moments together.

I am sick of irony. The other day, you kissed me at the very same place where I had arranged to meet him. I wondered who was right. Whether I knew where I was any more or whether it was you who entered our ephemeral story?

I scan years, deploy flashbacks and study gestures. I look to the sky to find out where destinies meet. Yearn for me, oh yearn for me or I will die of loneliness.

I want truth to convulse my whole body and rip open the straitjacket of my very flesh.

LXXXVI

You begin to love the big city of stone when it stirs memories; when one of its roads reminds you of someone you hold dear, or when one of its neighbourhoods reawakens a certain phase of your life. In a park you frequented before, you relive the past.

The big city turns beautiful under the snow. It looks like a newly-wed, and the joy that fills your heart is equal to nothing, other than the expanse of the sky.

You feel akin to peace. You want to laugh at life with its bad sense of humour, the delusion of being in control of your own existence.

Now, you need no longer think, tell lies or connive. All that remains is for you to live your life without hesitation.

LXXXVII

The postman comes twice, at eight in the morning and at one o'clock. He throws a bundle of letters through the front door. The bundle lands with a thud. I check to see if there is any mail for me. Stamps from my country.

I pick up the newspaper.

Here, there is a great deal of talk about South Africa. On the front pages, you see pictures of riots and funerals. Sad, morose, serious and defiant faces. You read long articles, and the same names and the same words keep cropping up: Nelson Mandela, Winnie, Desmond Tutu, Boesak, Oliver Tambo, the ANC, the UDF, passbooks, riots, imprisonment, trials, apartheid, anti-apartheid, impose economic sanctions or not?

But sometimes I say to myself, 'There, Africans are fighting, dying and I am doing nothing. My life sheltered in the heart of this city of stone. I just don't know, I just don't know.'

LXXXVIII

I have a courageous friend. I met him at university, and his strength amazes me. He is different from other blind people, with only the white part of their eyes visible. No, you can see his eyes, which are the colour of mine. The only way you can tell that he is blind is through his gaze which does not settle on anything.

I thought that he was born like that, without ever experiencing light, but I learned that it had all occurred one day.

He must have been twelve years old when it happened. He was playing in the yard. His mother was cooking the evening meal. Then everything went blank. I do not know the reason why. He has never told me. Nothing can be done, he cannot see.

Now he lives in the big city of stone. He left his vast country in Africa. And it is better for him, this exile. An exile where the inhabitants have respect for a white stick, where the state ensures his well-being and where facilities enable him to read and write.

It is just a question of money. A question of infrastructure.

LXXXIX

It is quite simple. I no longer recall the sensation of his touch. In any case, there is not much to be said. I can see that it is too difficult. I feel that this story cannot work. If he appeared now, I do not know what I would do. Throw my life out of the window, or turn my back on him?

It is not that complicated. It is either a great love, or a huge joke.

XC

I know for certain that I have nothing to reproach you with, that you are true to me. I know for certain that with every passing day, you give me a bit more, that you listen to my confusion and want to hear my laughter.

I know this for certain. It's just this apartment with its bright walls. Shutting the door cuts me off from the smell of earth. It's being cooped up in this space, just the two of us, watching each other's gestures, seeing words rebound and wound our souls. It's this television with meaningless words, the yelling matches. It is being on my own, in front of my typewriter, writing the days away and you, in the evenings, your back bent, while you eat.

I tell you all it takes is a strange noise from the radiator and my eyes stay peeled in the darkness of our bedroom. All it takes is the slightest intake of breath and my sleep leaps a hundred metres high.

Yet, just as the night begins to fall, when I am curled against your body that is as warm as a croissant, I have visions of happiness.

I can see us loving each other for a long time to come. We are here today, tomorrow we will be somewhere else where my body will find its rhythm and I will recognise the faces of passers-by.

XCI

With you I have rediscovered simple words, rediscovered the joy of evenings spent chatting, nights spent holding hands, hoping for a city that will not leave behind a bitter taste of defeat in the mornings.

Maybe together, we will make it.

Please do not reproach me for unleashing a storm upon this sleepy city, for mislaying dreams made of rare pearls and fetish gold.

XCII

He has lodged himself in my heart and I do not know what to do with him. But I do not want him to become a bad memory. I feel a richness pervading me. This love for you and for him.

Who knows? It may rot with time ... or flourish like a hibiscus in full bloom.

VÉRONIQUE TADJO was born in Paris and raised in Abidjan, Côte d'Ivoire. She has a BA in English from Abidjan University and a PhD in African American Literature and Civilization from the Sorbonne, Paris IV. She was a Fulbright Scholar at Howard University in Washington, DC, and a lecturer at Abidjan University for several years. Tadjo's body of work includes two collections of poetry: *Latérite* (Hatier, 1984), which won a literary award, and *A Mi-Chemin* (L'Harmattan, 2000). Her novels are: *Le Royaume Aveugle* (L'Harmattan, 1992), *À Vol d'Oiseau* (L'Harmattan, 1992), *Champs de Bataille et d'Amour* (Présence Africaine/Nouvelles Editions Ivoiriennes, 1999), *L'Ombre d'Imana* (Actes Sud, 2000), about the genocide in Rwanda, and *Reine Pokou* (Actes Sud, 2005), which won the Grand Prix Littéraire d'Afrique Noire. Her fiction has been published in 15 languages across the world. Tadjo has also written and illustrated several books for young people, edited a short anthology of African poetry called *Talking Drums* (A&C Black, 2000) and another of African stories and tales, *Chasing the Sun* (A&C Black, 2006). She is a prolific essayist and most of her work is available in English translations. Tadjo is currently the Head of French Studies at the University of the Witwatersrand, Johannesburg.

Kenyan-born **DR WANGŨI WA GORO** is a social critic, academic, writer and translator. She co-edited *Global Feminist Politics: Identities in a Changing World* (2000) with Suki Ali and Kelly Coate, and has performed her poetry in Africa, Europe and the USA. Her short stories 'Heaven and Earth' and 'Deep Sea Fishing' were published in the award-winning *Anthology of Love Stories* (2006). Her translations include Ngũgĩ wa Thiong'o's *Matigari* and his children's books, the Njamba Nene series, which she translated from Gikũyũ to English. She is currently working on a Gikũyũ translation of Boccaccio's *Il Decamerone*. As well as her keen interest in the development of African languages and literatures, Wangũi is involved in the promotion of literature and translation internationally and is the current president of the Translation Caucus of the African Literature Association, director of the Association for the Promotion of Translation in Relation to Africa and the deputy vice president of the African Literature Association.